BIRBAL THE CLEVER COURTIER

Anupa Lal has written more than twenty books for children. These include a retelling of the Ramayana, two books of poems, and translations of several short stories by the noted Hindi writer Premchand as well as his last novel *Godan*.

Birbal
the Clever Courtier

Retold by
Anupa Lal

SCHOLASTIC
New York Toronto London Auckland Sydney
Mexico City New Delhi Hong Kong Buenos Aires

Published by Scholastic India Pvt. Ltd.
A subsidiary of Scholastic Inc., New York, 10012 (USA).
Publishers since 1920, with international operations in Canada, Australia, New
Zealand, the United Kingdom, Mexico, India, Argentina and Hong Kong.

For information regarding permission, write to:
Scholastic India Pvt. Ltd.
Golf View Corporate Tower-A, 3rd Floor,
DLF Phase-V, Gurgaon 122002 (India)

Typeset by Mantra Virtual Services Pvt Ltd

First edition: June 2007
Reprinted by Scholastic India Pvt. Ltd; August; November 2007
January; August; November 2008; January 2009

10 Digit ISBN: 81-7655-815-X
13 Digit ISBN: 978-81-7655-815-0

Rs 100

Printed at Dot Scan, New Delhi

Contents

Foreword

These stories are among the many featuring Birbal, who was one of the cleverest and perhaps the favourite courtier of the Mughal Emperor Akbar. Although the various incidents related here may not actually have taken place in the India of the sixteenth century, these amusing and thought-provoking stories have entertained generations of listeners and readers.

They are a well-known and much loved part of Indian folklore, along with stories of other court jesters like Gopal Bhar and Tenali Raman.

The Clever Courtier

Akbar is one of the greatest kings of all time. Besides being a fearless warrior, he was also a man of intelligence and vision. If Akbar possessed a flaw, it was his vanity.

Akbar was tolerant towards all religions. One day, after listening to a discussion on the Ramayana, the Emperor declared that he was a reincarnation of Lord Rama! The Hindu pundits were horrified. Akbar was a great king, but how could a mere mortal—and a Muslim at that—claim to be an incarnation of Lord

Rama? The Emperor's false notion had to be rebuffed, but the question was how.

Mahesh Das was a young Brahmin with a sharp wit. He heard of the pundits' dilemma.

'Take me with you to the durbar tomorrow,' he pleaded. 'Perhaps I can convince Shahenshah Akbar that he is not Bhagwan Rama.' The pundits scoffed at the idea, but Mahesh Das was adamant.

'Who is this young lad?' the Emperor asked the pundits as Mahesh Das bowed before him in the court the following day. 'How is such a young boy, who has not a hair on his chin, in the company of learned men like you?

'If the Shah Alam judges a man's wisdom by the number of hairs on his chin, I can produce one who is wiser than us all!' said Mahesh Das.

Mahesh Das left the court and reappeared a few minutes later, leading a billy goat with a long beard!

The pundits shot anxious glances towards Akbar. Would he be angry at Mahesh Das's impertinence? But Akbar smiled.

'You are a small boy but your wits are sharp,' he said.

'If His Majesty would prefer someone large, I can bring in a camel or an elephant!' said Mahesh Das.

The pundits gasped. Surely this time Mahesh Das

had gone too far! But the Emperor burst out laughing.

'Be careful, my boy!' he said. 'That sharp tongue can get you into trouble.'

Akbar pointed to the jug full of water and the pile of stones that Mahesh Das had with him. 'What are these for?' he asked.

Mahesh Das approached the throne. 'Jahanpanah, I would like to make a humble request. Please throw these stones into the jug of water so that they land one on top of the other.'

The Emperor looked at the young Brahmin with a bemused expression on his face. Then he took the jug and the stones from him and proceeded to throw the stones into the water. Out of the lot, only two stones landed one on top of the other, the rest lay scattered about.

'That was more difficult than I thought,' Akbar commented.

'Alampanah, Lord Rama had a bridge built across the ocean, from India to Lanka, in a similar manner!' said Mahesh Das.

'So you are trying to prove that Lord Rama was a far greater man than your Emperor!' Akbar's voice was tinged with both annoyance and admiration. He turned to the pundits.

'This young lad is a far better pundit than all of you! We will make him a courtier. I enjoy the company of clever minds.' Then, looking at Mahesh Das, Akbar said, 'My young friend, what have you to say?'

Mahesh Das could not believe his good fortune! He bowed and said, 'Jahanpanah, I will serve you with my heart and soul.'

Mahesh Das soon came to be known as Birbal! And this is how he met Emperor Akbar for the first time.

The Six Fools

The Emperor was tired. He had been conversing with scholars and leaders of different religions for several hours.

'My head is heavy, Birbal,' he said when the scholars had departed. 'I wish to lighten it.'

'A few days of riding and hunting will refresh Your Majesty,' said Birbal.

'That of course,' said Akbar. 'But why not try a different amusement? Do you realise that as an Emperor I converse only with wise and capable men?

Let me meet some fools for a change!'

'Find the six most foolish men in the city, Birbal, and bring them to me. It seems ages since I had a hearty laugh! Six days to find the six greatest fools in Agra. Not too daunting a task for a man of your intelligence?'

Birbal hid a smile. 'No, Your Majesty,' he said. 'Fools are never in short supply.'

But Birbal soon discovered he was wrong. No one he met or was told about seemed foolish enough to be presented to the Emperor. Five days passed and the last day of his search dawned. Once again Birbal set off from home. Real fools were proving to be really elusive! He would have been more amused by this fact if he had been less anxious about his approaching deadline.

Birbal stopped to pluck a wild flower from a bush on the roadside when a man came running backwards and banged into him. Birbal staggered and almost fell.

'Forgive me, *huzoor*,' said the man. 'I did not see you. I am a muezzin. I call devotees to prayer in the mosque nearby.'

'But why are you running and that too backwards?' enquired Birbal.

'I am running with my voice, *huzoor*,' said the muezzin earnestly. 'I wish to see how far it carries.'

Birbal was delighted! He had found his first fool!

Keeping a straight face, he said, 'The Emperor will be happy to meet such a dedicated man. Come to the court tomorrow.'

Birbal continued on his way, smiling to himself. He had not gone much further when he saw a man on a donkey, holding a bundle of firewood high above his head.

'Your arms will get tired,' said Birbal as the man approached him. 'Why not rest your bundle on the back of your donkey?'

'The poor creature is already burdened by my weight, sarkar,' said the man. 'I cannot increase his burden.'

'That is indeed a generous thought,' said Birbal. He had found his second fool! 'Come to the court tomorrow. The Emperor will be happy to meet a noble soul like you.'

The afternoon sun was blazing down from the sky. Birbal had not encountered any more genuine fools. Feeling hot and thirsty, he walked towards a well in a nearby field and saw a man hard at work, digging. From the piles of freshly dug up earth it seemed as if the man was digging up the entire field!

Birbal satisfied his thirst with cool water from the well and then walked over to the labouring man.

'It seems as if you are searching for something,' said Birbal.

'*Ji huzoor*,' said the man. Sweat streamed down his face. 'I buried a bag full of gold coins in this field for safekeeping eight months ago. Now I'm digging it up. But I can't find it.'

'Surely you marked the spot where you buried your money,' said Birbal.

'I am not a fool, *huzoor*,' said the man indignantly. 'Of course I did. There was a big, black cloud in the sky, shaped just like an elephant. I buried my bag right under it. I don't know where the cloud has gone but I'll find my money even if I have to dig up the entire field!'

The man resumed digging and Birbal's eyes gleamed. He had found his third fool! Clapping the man on his shoulder, Birbal said, 'Our Emperor will be happy to reward a hardworking man like you. Come to the court tomorrow.'

Night had fallen by the time Birbal turned homewards. He had discovered only three of the greatest fools in the city. The Emperor had asked for six. A frown creased Birbal's forehead.

It was a bright, moonlit night. Birbal had almost reached home when, on a stretch of open ground lit by moonlight, he saw a man bending and examining the ground.

Birbal stopped. 'What are you doing?' he asked. 'Can I help you?'

'I am looking for my ring, *huzoor*,' said the man, still busy searching. 'I dropped it.' He straightened up to ease his aching back. 'I dropped it under that tree.' He pointed to a peepal tree nearby.

Birbal was startled. 'But my good man,' he said, 'if you dropped your ring there, why look for it here?'

'*Huzoor*, there is light here,' said the man patiently. 'There is no light there.'

'Of course!' said Birbal, smiling inwardly. 'Of course! Come to the court tomorrow. Our Emperor enjoys meeting intelligent men like you and he is generous with his gifts.'

He left the man looking surprised and happy. Birbal was happy too. He had found another fool!

The following day Birbal presented all four fools to the Emperor in court. Akbar listened with a straight face as Birbal related how he had met each one. All four were richly rewarded and sent home.

Akbar's eyes were twinkling as he turned to Birbal. 'You are right,' he said. 'These men are indeed four of the most precious fools in our kingdom! But I had asked you to search for six.'

'Jahanpanah,' said Birbal gravely, 'please count me as the fifth fool.'

Akbar raised his eyebrows in enquiry.

Birbal continued, 'For having devoted so much time and energy to this search.'

'Hmmm! I see!' said the Emperor after a pause. He looked at Birbal keenly. 'And the sixth fool? Where is he?'

Birbal bowed his head. There was pin-drop silence in court. Then, to Birbal's great relief, Akbar burst out laughing.

'Your Emperor is the sixth fool, is he not?' said Akbar. 'For sending you on such a wild-goose chase?'

The entire court laughed along with the Emperor. 'All this foolishness has refreshed me greatly!' said Akbar with a broad smile. 'Thanks to you, Birbal! And now, let us attend to matters of state ...'

The Three Statues

Birbal had not been to Akbar's court for several days. Courtiers like Mulla do Piaza, who resented Birbal's influence over Akbar, had managed to poison Akbar's mind against him. 'It was Birbal who was behind the latest rebellion,' they whispered into the Emperor's ears. 'Birbal had betrayed the Emperor's confidence … Birbal was a traitor,' they insinuated.

Akbar said nothing to Birbal about these allegations. There was, after all, no proof. But Birbal sensed the distrust and suspicion creeping into the

Emperor's mind and thought it wise to keep out of his way.

Days passed. Akbar began to miss his quick-witted and intelligent adviser. But Birbal continued to stay away.

One morning a master craftsman came to the *diwan-i-aam* with an exquisite gift for the Emperor— three identical statues made of pure gold.

'They are beautiful!' said Akbar. 'And absolutely alike!'

The craftsman shook his head. 'They are not entirely alike, Your Majesty, and one is superior to the other two. But it needs a very keen eye and a keen mind to spot what is different in each one.'

The statues were passed from hand to hand, but not one of the courtiers present, nor the Emperor himself, could spot any difference in the statues.

'Only one man can do what we have not been able to,' declared the Emperor. 'Send for Birbal.'

Minutes later, Birbal entered and bowed low before his king. 'I cannot believe this man is treacherous,' thought the Emperor. 'The sight of him gladdens my heart!'

'Look closely at these three statues, Birbal' said Akbar. 'Are they different from one another or are they exactly the same? If they are different, which one of the three, in your opinion, is the best?'

Birbal inspected the statues for several minutes. Then he sent for a fine metal wire and inserted it through a tiny hole he had discovered in the left ear of each statue.

In the case of the first statue, the wire came out through the right ear. In the second statue, the wire emerged through the mouth. In the third statue, the wire went in through the left ear, down into the stomach, and did not emerge at all.

'Your Majesty,' said Birbal, looking straight at Akbar for the first time since he had entered the court, 'these three statues may look alike, but they are very different. Let us compare them to three kinds of advisers.

'The first one hears what his monarch says to him in confidence, but is either too dull or too inattentive to retain anything. Whatever he hears goes in through one ear and out through the other.

'The second adviser hears what his monarch says, but blurts it out at the first opportunity. No secret is safe with him.

'The third adviser hears what his monarch says and keeps it to himself. He neither forgets what he hears nor betrays the king's trust in him.

'In my humble opinion, Your Majesty, the third adviser is the best. So the third statue, with only one hole, is the finest of the three.'

Akbar looked at the master craftsman who had made the three statues. 'That is absolutely correct, Your Majesty,' he said.

'Birbal,' said the Emperor, with deep affection in his voice, 'you possess not just a keen eye and a keen mind, but also a good and faithful heart. These three statues are yours. Take them as a small token of our great esteem for your abilities.'

Man versus Destiny

The royal boat raced through the dark waters of the Yamuna as buoyantly as a bird in flight. Stars twinkled in the night sky. The Emperor leaned back and paused, the oars resting in his hands. His face was flushed after several minutes of vigorous rowing. He let the oarsman replace him and came back to his seat.

'Shah Alam handles the boat with as much ease and wisdom as he handles the destiny of Hindustan,' said Abul Fazal.

'What is destiny?' Akbar mused aloud. 'Man makes his own destiny with the power of his mind and the power in his hands. Destiny is only clay which man must mould and shape.'

'Let us not underestimate destiny, My Lord,' said Birbal. 'It is destiny that shapes our lives; not we who control destiny. Destiny is infinitely stronger than us.'

'Birbal!' Akbar protested, 'I did not expect such a lame and cowardly opinion from you!'

'I spoke the truth, my lord—unpalatable though it may be.'

Akbar's heavy brows came together in a frown. He pulled off a sparkling diamond and ruby ring from the little finger of his left hand. He held up the ring for all the courtiers to see. Then, very deliberately he threw the ring down into the depths of the river!

'Birbal,' said the Emperor, 'I want that ring returned to me in three days. You believe that destiny is all-powerful. So if your destiny is good, the ring will be recovered. And if your destiny is bad, you will lose your head three days from now. Well? What have you to say?'

'Nothing, My Lord,' said Birbal quietly. 'I trust in destiny.'

Mulla do Piaza and Shahbaz Khan exchanged triumphant looks.

'Farewell, Birbal,' said Mulla do Piaza softly. 'I

fear your days in this world are numbered.'

Birbal began to fear the same thing himself. His wife, his children and his relatives all upbraided him.

'Why must you always contradict the Emperor?' his wife wept angry tears. 'Now he will have your head cut off. And then what will become of us?'

'Who knows what fate has in store for us?' Birbal said stoically. 'Compose yourself and trust in destiny. No one can change the hour of his death.'

Birbal waited for the three days to pass. There was nothing he could do to recover the ring. In his mind, he prepared himself for the execution which had been fixed for two in the afternoon.

At noon on the third day, the Emperor sent for Birbal. Akbar was having his lunch. He had only one meal in a day, and that meal was sumptuous. An array of some sixty dishes—served in plates of gold, silver, stone, and china—was brought before the Emperor. Each dish was tied in fine linen cloth, and sealed and labelled before it came into Akbar's presence.

The Emperor ate sparingly. 'Birbal, my friend,' said Akbar, 'destiny has let you down.' He helped himself to a dish of *zard birinj*. 'My ring still lies at the bottom of the river. I fear your foolish head must feel the bite of the executioner's axe in less than two hours from now. But it is not too late. I do not want to lose you. Take back your words and we will forget the whole business.'

There was a minute's silence as the *mir bahawal* laid a dish of curried fish before the Emperor.

Then Birbal shook his head. Much to his own surprise, he heard himself say, 'I cannot take back my words, Alampanah. I do believe in destiny. If the hour of my death has come, there is nothing you or I can do about it.'

Akbar was greatly perturbed. 'Birbal, you are a— THHOOO!' The Emperor spat out a mouthful of fish. The terrified *mir bahawal* almost collapsed!

'A fish full of stones!' thundered Akbar. 'I almost cracked my teeth on one! Guards, have this man flogged and—' Akbar forgot to complete his sentence. He was staring at the 'stone' he had spat out with the fish.

'Birbal!' shouted the Emperor. 'Look here! Look here! My ring! Destiny has saved you after all! You were right, Birbal. As always, you were right! Guards, release the man. He is an agent of destiny. He served me the only fish in the Yamuna that had swallowed the Emperor's ring! Birbal, I have not lost you after all! Destiny is great, my friend. Let us salute your destiny!'

The Ride to Shivpuri

One day, Birbal sat despondently with an untouched plate of food in front of him. His wife was trying unsuccessfully to get him to eat.

'I'm not hungry,' Birbal muttered as he hit out irritably at a mosquito that was droning in his ear.

'But you must eat something,' insisted his wife. 'You have not touched a morsel of food the whole day!'

'I know! I know!' Birbal shook his head in exasperation. 'Tell me, why doesn't the Emperor use the remarkable brain that Allah has given him? Listen to this. Yesterday, Raja Todar Mal suggested that if I were really clever, I should be able to relate an incident that never happened, that is not happening, and that will never happen! Todar Mal dislikes me and the Emperor knows it! But he agreed with him and said, "Birbal, I give you two weeks. Think of a suitable incident or admit that you are a fool!"'

'At least he didn't say he would have your head cut off!' Birbal's wife tried to console him. She was thinking of the time Akbar had told Birbal to recover his ring from the Yamuna.

'Please eat,' she said. 'I will pray to Lord Shiva. He will help you to satisfy the Emperor.'

'What can Lord Shiva—' Birbal began and then stopped. Raja Todar Mal's devotion to Lord Shiva was well known. A thought crept into Birbal's mind and began to grow into a plan. His eyes gleamed. He pulled the plate closer and began to eat.

It was well past midnight. Raja Todar Mal sat praying in the candle-lit Shiva temple he had built outside his house. The tinkling of a bell broke into his meditation. He turned and stood transfixed with amazement! It was Lord Shiva himself! Even in the darkness, Todar Mal could see Lord Shiva's piercing eyes, ash-smeared body and matted locks. He stood there with the trident in his hand, the snake coiled around his neck, and the Nandi bull by his side. It was the bell around Nandi's neck that had tinkled softly.

Raja Todar Mal threw himself at Lord Shiva's feet.

Birbal scratched his neck. A dead snake was an uncomfortable necklace! But Birbal was pleased with himself. Todar Mal had not recognised him—so far, at any rate!

'My son,' said Birbal, in what he hoped was a god-like voice, 'you have been a good and faithful devotee of mine for several years. I have come to reward you. Give up this life of toil and care. Come with me to Shivpuri—the abode of eternal bliss!'

A look of ecstasy came over Todar Mal's face. 'My Lord,' he said in a voice choked with emotion, 'I cannot believe my good fortune! My happiness overwhelms me. But ... but I beg you for a day's leave. Just one day to bid farewell to my Emperor and my family.'

'Your wish is granted,' said Birbal. 'Be here at the same time tomorrow night.' He turned and strode off into the darkness, the placid Nandi by his side.

'Ah, what a fantastic *baazi*! *Shabaash*! *Mohana*! *Shabaash*!'

The chief of the imperial pigeons flew straight down into the Emperor's hands after performing the most intricate acrobatics in the air. Akbar caressed her soft feathers and turned to Raja Todar Mal.

'My faithful *diwan*,' he said, 'you look all flushed and excited. I know it is not pigeon-flying that brings such a colour to your cheeks! What good news are you concealing? Tell me.'

Birbal stood a short distance away. He could not hear what Todar Mal was telling the Emperor. But he could guess. Akbar was looking at Todar Mal a little quizzically. Suddenly, the Emperor caught Birbal's eye. Akbar looked at Todar Mal and back again at Birbal. He knew his wily minister! Especially when he was up to some mischief!

Once again, it was well past midnight. Raja Todar Mal stood outside the Shiva temple, his hands folded, waiting anxiously. A bell tinkled softly in the darkness. Within seconds, Lord Shiva appeared. Raja Todar Mal prostrated himself at Shiva's feet.

'Come, my son,' said Birbal. 'The road to Shivpuri is fraught with danger. Human eyes cannot bear to see the horrors along the way. So you must hide yourself in this sack and keep very quiet. Evil spirits may pinch and prod you as we proceed. But fix your mind on Shivpuri and your sufferings will seem nothing.'

Raja Todar Mal obediently climbed into a large sack. Birbal had made many small holes in the sack for Todar Mal to breathe. The sack was loaded on to Nandi the bull, and the journey to Shivpuri began.

As they left Todar Mal's house, Birbal suddenly felt as if someone was watching them. But when he turned, there was no one. For two hours, the bull wandered through the streets of Agra with Todar Mal slung across his back. Occasionally, Birbal would pinch the body in the sack, or slap it across the buttocks. But Todar Mal kept heroically silent! More than once, Birbal thought he heard someone smothering a laugh, but no one was visible.

As dawn was breaking, Birbal led his bull to Agra's *subzi mandi*. It was deserted. He lifted the sack and deposited it near one of the vegetable stalls. Then he went home.

Half an hour later, the *mandi* came to life, and was filled with noise and bustle.

'*Arrey*! What is this?' one vegetable-seller asked another. He gave the sack a kick. Todar Mal winced.

'Seems like a sack of rotten melons!' the other man answered, giving the sack another kick.

Raja Todar Mal could bear it no longer. He forgot about reaching Shivpuri!

'Open the sack, you rascals!' he roared. 'I'll show you what rotten melons it contains!'

Late that evening, Akbar sat in the *diwan-i-khas* with a few chosen courtiers.

'Well, Birbal,' he said, 'two weeks are over. You were to tell us something that never happened, that is not happening, and that would never happen. Is your answer ready, or do you admit defeat?'

Birbal was silent. Raja Todar Mal looked at the Emperor with a smug look on his face.

Then Birbal spoke. 'Shah Alam, let us imagine—just for a second—that Raja Todar Mal was to be bundled in a sack and loaded on to a bull!'

Everyone present burst out laughing! Only Raja Todar Mal looked uncomfortable.

Birbal continued, 'And let us suppose he thought that he was on his way to Shivpuri, the abode of eternal bliss! But he got no further than Agra's *subzi mandi*! Could such a thing ever happen?'

Raja Todar Mal was furious! But he also realised that he could not say anything without giving himself away.

'My clever Birbal,' said the Emperor softly. 'You have proved your worth once again.' He yawned. 'I shall sleep well tonight. Wandering through the streets of Agra can be tiring for a man of my age!'

Hairless Palms

The Emperor had just returned from a good hunt and was sitting contentedly with his courtiers in the *diwan-i-khas*, the hall of private audience, at Fatehpur Sikri.

Akbar was in an indulgent mood. Turning towards Birbal, he said affectionately, 'Birbal, you are a clever man.' Then without waiting for a response, he repeated, 'Yes, you are a clever man; everyone knows that.'

Birbal bowed his head in acknowledgement of

the king's praise. 'But even you do not know the answer to every question. Or do you?' Akbar asked in a challenging tone. He slapped his hand down, palm upwards, on the scarlet Persian carpet and then asked Birbal, 'Why is my palm hairless? I have hair on every other part of my body, then why not on my palm? Can you tell me why?'

Once he had finished, Akbar leaned back on his throne feeling pleased with himself. Birbal was silent.

Mulla do Piaza dug his elbow into Raja Todar Mal's ribs and murmured, 'Our clever Birbal seems to be in a fix this time!'

'May I answer your question, Alampanah?' Birbal asked.

'By all means,' Akbar replied.

'My Lord, you are the most munificent of rulers! There would not be a single poor or needy man who has not sung your praises. The palms of your gracious hands are so generous. An endless stream of coins passes through them. That is the reason why they are hairless. Hair has no chance to grow on your ever-bountiful palms!'

Akbar was both pleased and disappointed. Pleased at Birbal's clever reply and disappointed that Birbal had outwitted him yet again.

But the Emperor was not one to give in so easily. He said almost immediately. 'If it is as you say, Birbal, then why are your palms hairless too? You are not a great dispenser of charity!'

If Birbal was perplexed, it was only for a fraction of a second. He had his rejoinder ready soon enough: 'No doubt, I do not give, Your Majesty, but I do take!' he said holding out his palms. 'These palms are constant recipients of your great charity. Hair has no chance to grow on these either!'

'It is no use,' Akbar said to himself resignedly, 'Birbal always manages to outwit me.' Even so, he could not resist asking a third question.

With a sidelong glance at the others present, Akbar said, 'Birbal, perhaps you are right. But, tell me, why do my other courtiers have hairless palms too?'

This time Birbal was silent for two whole minutes! Akbar was triumphant. 'I've got him finally!' thought the Emperor. Mulla do Piaza nudged Todar Mal again.

Then Birbal cleared his throat. 'Jahanpanah,' he said, looking embarrassed, 'it is not my intention to speak disparagingly of my fellow courtiers, yet, I must answer your question. Well, Your Majesty, the reason they have no hair on their palms is simple: they are so busy wringing their hands in jealousy and dismay at the generosity you bestow on me that hair has no chance to grow on their palms either.'

The *diwan-i-khas* resounded with Akbar's laughter. He leaned forward and patted Birbal on the shoulder.

'Birbal, you are one in a million,' Akbar said admiringly. 'I would not exchange a man of your wit for all the coins in my treasury.'

The Precious Relics

The Emperor was engaged in an endless discussion with two Portuguese priests who were visiting the court. Akbar's intelligent observations matched the eloquence of the priests. The discussion carried on late into the night.

Birbal was overcome with drowsiness. As he stifled his umpteenth yawn, Akbar shot him a reproving look. The Emperor himself was tireless.

'So you see, Birbal, my tired friend,' the Emperor said indulgently, 'how great is Allah! Our esteemed guests may call him by another name, but that makes no difference, Allah is supreme, He is all-powerful.'

'There is something more powerful than Allah, My Lord!' Birbal said suddenly.

'More powerful than Allah? And what is that, Birbal?' Akbar's eyes gleamed at the prospect of another argument.

'Belief, Jahanpanah. Belief is stronger than even Allah!'

'Birbal, you put the cart before the horse!' Akbar smiled.

'Sleep has affected Birbal's wits, Your Majesty,' Mulla do Piaza said maliciously.

'Give me two months and I will prove what I just said.' Birbal's voice was calm and self-assured. He did not seem sleepy at all!

The next day, Birbal set to work. He had a small shrine constructed half a mile from Fatehpur Sikri and appointed a priest to look after the shrine.

Next, he acquired a pair of the Emperor's sandals. Wrapping the sandals in a plain woollen shawl he placed them in the shrine as holy relics.

Soon people began to gather near the shrine. Everyone wanted to know whose shrine it was. The priest had been instructed by Birbal to inform the people that it was the shrine of Saint Abdul Karim, a pious and holy man who had died while on pilgrimage to Mecca a few months ago. He also told the people that the saint had performed extraordinary miracles in his lifetime, and his precious relics could still perform wonders for those who believed in them.

As expected, the people listened and believed. They brought their problems to the shrine and prayed for solutions. Some of the problems did find solutions. Some of the sick did get better. As its fame spread, people from far off places came to pray at the shrine of the mythical Saint Abdul Karim!

By the time word of the great shrine reached the Emperor's ears, the two months were almost over.

'I am told that just a glimpse of the precious relics can transform one's life!' Akbar said to Birbal one afternoon. 'Come Birbal, let us go and see this wondrous sight for ourselves. Great is the glory of Allah, Birbal—although you disagree, do you not?'

Not waiting for an answer, Akbar asked Birbal, 'Where is the proof of the claim that you made two months ago?'

'Shah Alam, it is almost ready,' Birbal murmured. 'Almost ready.'

On reaching the shrine, Akbar closed his eyes in reverence and prostrated himself before the shrine. When he stood up and opened his eyes, he saw Birbal wearing a contrite expression on his face and holding the holy relics in his hand.

'Forgive me, Jahanpanah,' said Birbal, before Akbar could utter a word of protest. 'I had to invent a saint and create a shrine in order to prove my point. These precious relics are nothing more than ...' He unwrapped the shawl, and the startled Emperor beheld his own sandals!

'Belief is all-powerful, My Lord,' Birbal continued. 'People believed these sandals were the relics of a saint, and so these very sandals performed miracles for them! Belief is greater than even Allah.'

The Emperor did not know whether to praise Birbal or be exasperated!

The Worth of a Beard

One day, after an unsuccessful hunting trip the Emperor said dejectedly, 'I am getting old, Birbal. Old age weakens the mind and destroys the body. I would willingly part with half the wealth of my kingdom to be young again!'

Birbal looked horrified. 'Half the wealth of your great kingdom for the immaturity and shallowness of a young mind! Maturity and wisdom come with age, Jahanpanah, and they are jewels beyond price!'

Akbar smiled. 'So you would back an old fox

against a young tiger, would you, Birbal?'

'Every time, Your Majesty,' Birbal said solemnly. 'Give me a few days and I will prove the truth of my assertion.'

Two days later, the Emperor was returning to the palace after another hunt. This time, several deer had fallen prey to Akbar's arrows and His Majesty was in a good mood!

Farmers were working in their fields by the wayside as the king's party passed by. Birbal summoned one of the farmers—a young man with a bushy black beard.

'Shahenshah Akbar would like to buy your beard,' Birbal said to the young farmer. 'What is your price?'

The farmer, the members of the hunting party, and the Emperor himself gaped at Birbal!

'Ten gold *mohurs* for your beard. Will that satisfy you?' Birbal asked briskly.

The astounded farmer could only nod his head. 'Come to the durbar tomorrow morning. We will take your beard and give you your money,' said Birbal.

Akbar fingered his chin thoughtfully as they continued on their way. 'Did I ask you to buy a beard for me, Birbal?' he asked. 'I think I am capable of growing one without spending even a paisa!'

'I beg for a little patience from Your Majesty,' said Birbal. 'If you remember our argument about youth and age …'

'A-ha!' said the Emperor. 'Are you trying to prove that there is no fool like a young fool? I fear, Birbal, that in this case you are more of a fool than the young farmer!'

'Jahanpanah, I have not finished. I have yet to prove my point,' replied Birbal. 'May I have your permission to bring an aged man to the durbar the day after tomorrow?'

'Yes, but on one condition. I will select the old man myself,' said the Emperor.

'Certainly, Shah Alam,' said Birbal. 'But please select one with a beard.'

The hunting party rode on. Akbar halted a short distance ahead, and pointed to a frail, old man smoking a hookah in the shade of a tree. The old man had a long white beard.

'I select him,' said the Emperor. 'Tell him to come to the durbar two days from today.'

.The young farmer came to the court the next morning. He was shaved by the king's barber. He left his beard behind and went home happily with the ten gold *mohurs* in his purse!

The frail old man whom Akbar had selected came to the court the day after. He offered *tasleem* to the Emperor and stood meekly in a corner, waiting to be summoned.

'The Emperor would like to buy your beard, old man,' said Birbal. 'How much is it worth?'

The old man was silent for a minute. Then he looked at Birbal gravely and said, 'Sarkar, my beard is my most precious possession! It has been my companion for many years and it has saved my honour on many occasions. Twelve years ago, a son was born to me after three daughters. My relations and my friends urged me to give a feast. But I am a poor farmer—I had no money. I went to a money lender and begged him for a loan of two gold *mohurs*. He looked at my beard and said, "You seem to be a respectable man! I will loan you the money."'

'*Huzoor,* my daughters grew up and I arranged marriages for them. Each time, I had to go to a moneylender and borrow thirty gold *mohurs* for the wedding expenses. I am a poor man, *sarkar*. If it were not for this beard of mine, I could not have done anything for my family! You ask me how much my beard is worth. *Huzoor,* it is a question of simple calculation. My beard is worth at least ninety-two gold *mohurs*!'

The court gaped. Even Birbal looked stunned!

Akbar grinned. 'You are right, old man. Your beard is very valuable indeed! We will pay you a hundred gold mohurs for it. Birbal, send for the barber.'

The barber approached the old man with a pair of scissors in his hand.

'Stop!' cried the old man. 'Don't you dare touch this beard. It is the sacred property of the Emperor!'

Akbar burst out laughing. 'You win, Birbal— you win!' he gasped. 'This man has more brains in his head than he has white hairs in his beard!' Akbar tossed a bag of *mohurs* to him. 'Here, old man, take your money and keep your beard. You can go.'

A fortnight later, Akbar continued to talk about the clever old man who had sold his beard for a hundred gold *mohurs* and still retained it on his chin.

Birbal entered the *Khwabgah* late one evening to find the Emperor chuckling over a letter he had received. It was from the same old man. It said that he was having a hard time maintaining the royal beard on his chin! Because it was the Emperor's property, he was careful to keep it cleaned, combed and oiled at all times. This left him very little time to farm his land. He requested the Emperor to grant him a sum of one gold *mohur* a month so he could make both ends meet!

'Tell Raja Todar Mal to have the money sent to the old man every month,' Akbar said to Birbal. 'He may be a rascal, but he is clever! Old age may have weakened his body, but his mind is as sharp as my sword blade!'

The old farmer began to receive his monthly salary to pay for the upkeep of the royal beard! News of his good fortune spread, and a few days later, an indignant clean-shaven young farmer burst into the court to protest.

'Jahanpanah, I sold you a brand new, black and beautiful beard for only ten gold *mohurs*. That old rascal Sadiq Ali sold his old white beard for a hundred! The beard is still on his chin and he is living like a lord! This is injustice, Shah Alam—I demand my beard back!'

Akbar shook his head sadly. 'There is really no fool like a young fool!' he said. 'Birbal, give this angry young man his beard and take back the *mohurs*!'

Hang My Son-in-law

One grey, overcast January morning Akbar was in a foul mood. He paced around restlessly in the *khwabgah*.

As soon as Birbal entered, Akbar said loudly, 'Birbal, sons-in-law are unnecessary people. All sons-in-law, including mine!'

Birbal was amused, but he kept a straight face. He was used to the Emperor's fits of anger and his unjustified declarations.

Then Akbar said grimly, 'I want all the sons-in-law in my kingdom put to death. Birbal, I command you to see that this is done,' he added.

Birbal was shocked! Akbar seemed to be in a far greater temper than usual, he thought. But he knew better than to argue with the king when he was in such a mood.

So, bowing his head, he said softly, 'It shall be done, Jahanpanah.'

A few days later, Akbar asked Birbal if his command had been carried out. Birbal begged the Emperor for some more time to complete the arrangements.

Three weeks later, Akbar again asked impatiently, 'So Birbal, are your arrangements still not complete?'

Again Birbal meekly requested more time, 'Please, Shah Alam, a few days more.'

Another week passed by. Akbar had run out of patience. 'I am not going to wait any more, Birbal,' he announced. 'I have had enough of your excuses, now I want to see results.'

Without uttering a word, Birbal led Akbar to a field outside the precincts of Fatehpur Sikri. Hundreds of scaffolds had been erected in the field, some made of wood, others of metal.

Akbar and Birbal began to walk around the field examining the different scaffolds. Most of the scaffolds were made of inferior quality wood. 'Who are these for?' Emperor Akbar asked.

'Jahanpanah, these are for the sons-in-law of the poor,' Birbal answered.

'And what about these?' Akbar asked, pointing to the scaffolds made of good teak wood. 'These are for the sons-in-law of the rich,' Birbal replied.

Then pointing to the third set of scaffolds, Akbar asked, 'And the ones made of brass and copper, who are they for?'

'They are for your courtiers,' Birbal answered.

By the time Akbar and Birbal reached the last lot of scaffolds, they had covered almost the entire field. Only eight scaffolds remained. Seven in shining silver and one in gleaming gold.

Akbar paused in front of the silver scaffolds. Before Akbar could say anything, Birbal informed him, 'These are for your sons-in-law, Alampanah.'

Akbar looked thoughtful, then pointing to the golden scaffold, he asked slowly, 'And, Birbal, who is this for?'

Birbal bowed his head. 'It is for the greatest son-in-law in the kingdom, My Lord.' Then his voice faltered as he went on, 'Jahanpanah, it is for you.'

The Emperor was left speechless. Birbal, on his part, wondered if his impertinence would cost him his head this time.

Then after a short, stunned silence, Akbar burst out laughing. 'Don't look so scared, Birbal,' he said, 'I have to thank you. I can always trust you to restore my good sense. Have these scaffolds dismantled immediately. We will not need them any more.'

The Ill Omen

One day, Emperor Akbar overslept. It was almost noon when he finally awoke and stumbled out of bed grumpily. The first person he saw was a sweeper cleaning the palace courtyard below. When the sweeper looked up and saw the Emperor, he prostrated himself on the ground in respect.

Akbar was most unhappy. Then several things happened in quick succession to make him unhappier still. First, he stumbled over a fold in the carpet as he walked across the room; then for the first time ever, the barber nicked Akbar's chin; this was followed by a ruby falling out of one of the Emperor's rings. And if this was not enough, the melons served to him at lunch were tasteless!

So much so that by the evening Akbar was in a really foul mood. When a messenger brought the news of the death of one of Akbar's distant cousins, it really was the last straw! Akbar could not control his temper any longer.

'Get out of my sight!' he roared at the terrified messenger. 'Birbal! Where is Birbal? Send Birbal to me at once.'

'Birbal!' Akbar shouted as soon as he saw his favourite minister. 'I have spent a miserable day. When I woke up this morning, the first face I saw was a sweeper's. Everything has gone wrong since. I want that sweeper put to death. Let his head be struck off at dawn tomorrow!'

'As you wish, Alampanah,' said Birbal quietly, and left the room.

When the sweeper learnt of the fate that awaited him, he fell at Birbal's feet and begged him to save his life.

'Only you can help me,' he wept. 'The Emperor will surely listen to you. I have done no wrong. If I die, who will look after my wife and children?'

'Dry your tears,' said Birbal, raising the sobbing

man to his feet. 'I will try my best to save you.'

The Emperor was up before dawn the next day. He said his prayers, and felt relaxed and refreshed.

There was a knock on the door. It was Birbal. Akbar suddenly remembered the order he had given.

'Come in, Birbal,' he said. 'Has that sweeper been executed yet?' he asked with a slight feeling of remorse.

'Everything is ready for the execution, Shah Alam,' Birbal replied. 'But the sweeper keeps repeating one thing, and I do not know how to refute it. Jahanpanah, the first person you saw yesterday was the sweeper. You considered that an ill omen and you had a bad day. But the first person the sweeper saw yesterday was Your Majesty. The sweeper claims that the sight of your face has been more unlucky for him than the sight of his face was for you! He is going to lose his life because the first person he saw yesterday was you.'

Birbal paused and looked at Akbar. The Emperor was silent.

'It is getting late. I shall tell the executioner to proceed,' said Birbal.

The Emperor raised his hand. 'Wait, Birbal,' he said. 'I have changed my mind. Let the sweeper go. He is right. His clever argument has saved his life. Or ... was it your brainwave? Come, come Birbal.

Do not pretend to look so innocent! I am not displeased. Tell the sweeper that his Emperor pardons him—thanks to your intervention!'

The Mango Tree

All was silent in the *diwan-i-aam*, the hall of public audience.

Two men stood in front of Emperor Akbar with their heads bowed. One a poor, thin and elderly farmer, the other a rich, plump, and middle-aged merchant. Both claimed to be innocent.

The Emperor addressed the poor farmer. 'You say that you left ten gold *mohurs* with this merchant before you went to your village, is that right?'

The farmer replied, 'Yes, Hazrat Salaamat.'

'He is lying, Jahanpanah!' interrupted the merchant.

Akbar glared at him and rebuked him sharply, 'Speak when you are spoken to.' Then turning to the farmer, he asked, 'Is it true that the merchant promised to keep your money safe till you returned?'

'That is right, Hazrat Salaamat,' the farmer said and continued, 'It is a long, dangerous way to the village. I did not want to carry the money in case I got robbed on the way.' With tears brimming in his eyes, he said, 'Alampanah, as soon as I returned yesterday I went to Makhan Ram and asked for my money. But, Makhan Ram denied outright that he had it and instead called me a liar.'

The farmer added, 'He turned me out of his house, Alampanah. Those ten *mohurs* were my lifetime's savings. I had been saving that money for a long time for the marriage of my daughter.'

'Don't weep, old man,' Akbar said gently. 'If you are telling the truth, you will get back your money.'

Then addressing the merchant, Akbar said, 'Now speak. What do you have to say?'

'Alampanah, this old fool Sharif Chand is a liar!' the merchant said angrily, his fat cheeks quivering with indignation. 'He did not leave any money with me. He just wants to cheat me out of ten gold *mohurs*, that is all.'

Akbar said thoughtfully, 'Sharif Chand, who else was present when you gave the money to Makhan Ram?'

'There was no one there, Jahanpanah, except for the mango tree under which we sat,' Sharif Chand said.

Akbar looked a little nonplussed. A murmur went around the courtroom and some of the courtiers smiled, but Birbal was silent.

'Your Majesty, may I say something to Sharif Chand?' Birbal asked.

'By all means,' Akbar replied, hopeful that Birbal might be able to sort out the wrangle in his inimitable style.

'Sharif Chand,' Birbal addressed the poor farmer, 'go to the mango tree and tell it to come to court as a witness.'

Everyone, including Akbar, was taken aback by the suggestion.

'But huzoor, the mango tree cannot move,' protested Sharif Chand.

'Go and do as you are told,' Birbal said firmly.

The old farmer left the court. Birbal instructed a soldier to follow him unseen.

Time passed. The Emperor, meanwhile, dealt with and dispensed justice in other cases. Birbal, on his part, watched the face of Makhan Ram carefully.

The plump merchant kept darting furtive glances towards the entrance. As time went by, he became increasingly nervous and fidgety.

Over an hour later, Sharif Chand returned to court, looking extremely dejected. He was alone. Makhan Ram was visibly relieved.

Sharif Chand fell at Birbal's feet. 'I begged and pleaded, *huzoor*, but the mango tree refused to move! I tried my best, I really did.'

The soldier who had been tailing the poor farmer, whispered in Birbal's ear, 'He is telling the truth, Your Honour. I saw him pleading with the tree.'

Birbal said reassuringly to Sharif Chand, 'Don't be disheartened. We know the truth. The mango tree came to the court after you visited it. It narrated the entire incident to us.'

Makhan Ram was stupefied. 'That is a lie, *huzoor*,' he shouted. 'The mango tree never came to the court. I did not see it.'

'Greed has clouded your vision, Makhan Ram,' Birbal said sternly. 'We have ways of uncovering the truth. Confess your guilt or your punishment will be doubled. Did you or did you not steal Sharif Chand's ten gold *mohurs*?'

Makhan Ram turned pale with fear. He bowed his head in shame, and admitted his guilt.

Makhan Ram was sentenced to six months'

imprisonment. Sharif Chand returned home triumphantly clutching his gold *mohurs*.

Finally, unable to restrain himself any longer Akbar turned to Birbal and said, 'The mango tree said something to me too, Birbal. It told me I was very lucky I had a minister who was clever enough to understand the language of trees!'

Pat came Birbal's reply: 'Your Majesty, you did not hear the tree's last remark. It claimed such unusual things happened only in the reign of a great and unusual king like Shahenshah Akbar!'

Shorten It

It was a balmy evening in March. Akbar was strolling in the red sandstone courtyard outside the *diwan-i-khas*. He had just completed a successful military campaign in the east.

Suddenly, Akbar turned to his courtiers and said, 'Tell me, what should be the punishment for someone who dared to tweak your Emperor's moustache?'

The courtiers were dumbfounded. Then Shahbaz Khan spoke up. 'Jahanpanah, he should be mercilessly flogged to death!'

'Beheaded in full public view, Your Honour!' said Mulla do Piaza.

'The villain should be thrown down from the ramparts of the fort and then hanged!' said Shadi Shah.

'And you, Birbal? What punishment do you suggest for this offender?' asked the Emperor.

'Shah Alam,' said Birbal calmly, 'I would give him some sweets.'

The other courtiers gaped at Birbal. Had he gone mad? Sweets for such a heinous crime? Surely this time Birbal would pay for his insolence!

Akbar frowned. 'Did I hear you right, Birbal?' he said. 'You consider sweets an appropriate punishment for such a crime?'

'Only in this case, Your Majesty,' said Birbal humbly. 'Who else but your beloved grandson would dare to take such a liberty with the king of kings?'

Akbar burst out laughing! 'It was indeed the little rascal!' he said. 'And I gave him sweets for his impertinence. Birbal, as usual you were right!'

The other courtiers laughed along with the Emperor even as they glared at Birbal for having upstaged them.

The stroll continued …

Then Akbar bent to pick up a small sharp stone. With it he drew a line on the ground and said, 'Birbal, you understood a child's mind and solved that little mystery. Here is an even simpler task for you to perform. Shorten this line.' He paused and there was a glint of mischief in the Emperor's eyes. 'But don't touch it. Just shorten it.'

Mulla do Piaza and Shahbaz Khan looked at each other and smirked. How would their arch rival shorten a line without touching it? This time he would have to admit defeat.

If Birbal hesitated, it was only for a moment. Then he bent down to pick up the stone that the Emperor had just discarded. With it he drew a longer line below the one that Akbar had drawn. All those present looked down at the two lines. The Emperor's line was clearly shorter than Birbal's!

There was a brief silence. Then Akbar smiled and said, 'I thought I had outwitted you this time, Birbal. I see I was wrong!'

A few weeks later Akbar left Agra on another expedition. The Emperor rode on an elephant and Birbal rode with him. The sun was strong and the journey long and arduous. Even after several hours, their destination was nowhere in sight.

'Birbal,' said the Emperor, wiping the sweat from his brow, 'I remember how you shortened the line I drew that evening. My ever-resourceful friend, can you not shorten our road today?'

Birbal knew there was no shorter road to their destination. But he bowed his head and said, 'Alampanah, your wish is my command. With your permission, may I just relate a short story about four princes who ...' Birbal launched into an intriguing tale to which Akbar listened intently. Before his interest could flag in one story, Birbal told him another, and another ...

Time flew and suddenly their destination lay before them! Akbar stretched his cramped limbs. 'What would I do without you, Birbal?' he said affectionately. 'You even managed to shorten a road for your Emperor! Here, take this!' Akbar pulled a diamond ring off his finger. 'You may shorten roads and lines, but may nothing, Inshallah, ever shorten our association!'

The Piece of Rope

It was a pleasant evening in April. Akbar was pacing
up and down along the ramparts of the fort. He was
followed by his courtiers, among them Shahbaz Khan
and Mulla do Piaza, doing what they did best—
criticising Birbal. Although they were speaking in
hushed tones, Akbar overheard snatches of their
conversation and ticked them off angrily. 'Shahbaz
Khan, enough of that malicious talk. I know you feel
I favour Birbal above all others, but I have good
reason to.'

Shahbaz Khan and Mulla do Piaza looked at each other sceptically. Akbar caught the look. With one furious movement, he bent down and picked up a short piece of rope that lay in a corner.

'Here!' He thrust the rope at Shahbaz Khan. 'Take this and sell it for a hundred gold *mohurs*.'

Shahbaz Khan gaped at the Emperor. 'Sell this— this piece of rope for one hundred gold *mohurs*, Your Majesty?' he squeaked.

'Exactly,' said Akbar calmly, with a gleam of triumph in his eyes. 'A simple task! Birbal could have done it in half a day! But I am giving you a whole week. Well? What are you waiting for? You have your merchandise; go sell it!'

The stunned courtier offered *tasleem* and took his leave. Akbar leaned over the wall and looked down at the empty space between the fort and the river Yamuna. He clapped his hands. 'Bring on the elephants!' called the Emperor.

Two huge, magnificent elephants lumbered towards each other and crashed head-on.

'I love a good fight,' the Emperor said contentedly, as he settled down to watch. 'Strength against strength; mind against mind.'

Shahbaz Khan lost badly in the battle of wits arranged by Akbar. He could not sell the piece of rope even for one gold *mohur*, leave alone a hundred!

Mulla do Piaza tried and so did some others, but they were all equally unsuccessful.

Birbal was away while all this took place. When he returned to Agra, Todar Mal told him the whole story.

'The Emperor claimed that *you* could sell the rope for a hundred gold mohurs in half a day!' said Raja Todar Mal.

If Birbal was taken aback, he did not show it. 'His Majesty reposes great trust in my humble abilities,' he said quietly. 'I must not betray his trust.'

The next morning, in the durbar hall—much to Akbar's delight—Birbal asked him for a piece of rope. He also asked that two court officials be allowed to accompany him.

Birbal went out of the palace towards the houses of the rich citizens of Agra. He stopped outside a large house and pretended to measure the boundary wall with the piece of rope. The guard at the gate informed the owner of the house of Birbal's presence.

'His Majesty is thinking of having a mosque built here,' Birbal told the owner of the house. 'All these houses will be pulled down. I am inspecting the area and taking the necessary measurements.'

The owner of the house was shocked to hear this. 'Please, please save my house,' he begged. 'It was built by my great-grandfather. We have lived here for three generations! You are a favourite with the Emperor. If you tell him this area is unsuitable for a mosque, he will definitely listen. I will be ever grateful to you for your help.' He pressed a bag full of money into Birbal's hand.

Birbal took the money and nodded kindly. 'I will do what I can,' he said.

The entire performance was repeated at the next large house in the area. After five such visits, Birbal sat down to count the money he had collected so far. It was more than three hundred gold *mohurs*! He returned to the palace. The time was 1.00 p.m.

'Well! Shahbaz Khan, what have you to say now?' the Emperor asked triumphantly after Birbal had handed him the money. 'Spend less time being spiteful and more polishing your wits. They are very rusty!'

Akbar turned to his favourite courtier. 'Birbal, I never cease to marvel at your resourcefulness!' He handed the bags of money back to Birbal.

'Take these,' he said. 'A small token of my great admiration!'

The Tank of Milk

The Emperor had a new flatterer in court, Shadi Shah. The more Shadi Shah fawned upon Akbar, the greater was Birbal's discomfiture. Shadi Shah hung on Akbar's every word and gesture, and Akbar on his part revelled in the flattery.

Akbar's smug expression was beginning to unsettle Birbal and he said to himself, 'I flatter the Emperor too, but I do try to maintain a balance by puncturing his vanity as well! But Shadi Shah is trying to turn the Emperor into as big a fool as himself! He is trying to convince the Emperor that the world begins and ends with him!'

No doubt Shadi Shah was a good soldier and hunter, which was why he came to the Emperor's notice in the first place. But he was also ambitious, insincere and servile. Under normal circumstances, Akbar would have seen through such flattery. But this time he seemed to be enjoying Shadi Shah's company. So it was no wonder then that Birbal was unhappy.

One sultry night, tired of sitting in the *diwan-i-khas*, Akbar decided to take a short stroll. It was completely still outside. Not a leaf stirred. The Emperor stopped near the Anup Talao and asked Shadi Shah, 'Why is this tank empty?' Then with a gleam in his eye, he added, 'Had it been full of water, we could have bathed and cooled ourselves.'

The flatterer had got his opportunity and said quickly, 'Bathe in water? Allah forbid! His Majesty should bathe in milk. This tank should be filled with milk to make it a bath befitting His Majesty!'

Birbal suppressed a smile. The vision of the big strong Akbar, splashing around in a tank of milk was funny to say the least.

Turning to Shadi Shah, Birbal said, 'What an excellent idea, my friend! Why don't you arrange for the tank to be filled with milk?'

Shadi Shah was taken aback. 'B-but ...' he spluttered, 'how can I?'

'It is easily done', Birbal assured Shadi Shah, 'just issue a proclamation asking each resident of Fatehpur Sikri to bring a jug of milk and pour it into the tank.'

Then looking up at the dark, moonless sky thoughtfully, he added, 'The tank will be full by dawn. His Majesty can bathe in it after his meditations. But, I would like to add that a tank full of water would provide a much more refreshing bath than a tank full of milk.'

'No one asked for your opinion, Birbal,' Shadi Shah said with unmasked irritation. He was annoyed that Birbal had suggested how the tank could be filled with milk.

Birbal restrained himself, though he would have happily slapped Shadi Shah for his insolence.

Soon the proclamation was issued. Even as Akbar and his courtiers retired for the night, the surprised and sleepy residents of Fatehpur Sikri diligently lined up near the Anup Talao and emptied their jugs of milk into the tank.

Slowly the tank began to fill up.

Akbar was up at dawn the next day. After he finished his prayers, Shadi Shah, Birbal and the other courtiers were summoned to accompany him to the tank of milk.

But when they reached the Anup Talao a strange sight greeted them. Instead of milk, the tank was full of water!

Shadi Shah gaped at the tank in astonishment. But Birbal smiled in satisfaction. What had happened was just what he had expected!

A perturbed Akbar turned to Shadi Shah, 'Shut your mouth, Shadi Shah, before a fly goes into it.' Then noticing that Birbal was smiling, the Emperor said, 'Birbal, as usual you appear to know something that the rest of us do not. What is it?'

Shadi Shah, meanwhile, turned towards the guard who had been on duty at the tank and shouted, 'Why is this tank full of water and not milk?'

Trembling with fear, the guard stammered, 'I-I don't know, Your Honour. Every man who visited the tank in the night poured in a jugful. I could not see in the dark if it was milk or water.'

Then Birbal spoke up, 'Your Majesty, your subjects took advantage of the darkness. Each of them thought that in the dark no one would notice if he poured in water instead of milk; and that a jug of water in a tank of milk would not make a difference. Since, unfortunately, each of them had the same thought, so all of them poured in water instead of milk. They were not being disrespectful to their

Emperor, only clever.'

Akbar was convinced. Laying his hand affectionately on Birbal's shoulder, he said, 'But who can be cleverer than you, Birbal? You had known all along that the people would behave this way. And you were right. And, besides, who in his right mind would bathe in milk on such a hot day when cold water would be much more refreshing?'

Then turning his back on the glowering Shadi Shah, Akbar continued, 'I need you, Birbal. I need you to check me when I start talking or listening to nonsense. I hereby appoint you Minister of Common Sense!'

And Akbar's Minister of Common Sense was no longer unhappy!

The Genuine Sanyasi

Shahenshah Akbar was in a black mood. One of his trusted generals had betrayed him.

'I am surrounded by liars and cheats,' Akbar said bitterly. 'I doubt if there are ten honest men in my entire kingdom!'

The courtiers present in the *diwan-i-khas* looked at one another uneasily. Who had the courage to contradict the king even if it meant branding oneself a liar or cheat?

'Jahanpanah, if I may venture an opinion,' Birbal

said gently, 'the picture may not be so bleak. True, the rogues will always outnumber the saints ...'

'Saints!' Akbar roared with laughter, 'Birbal, I didn't realise you were so out of touch with reality. Find me just one saintly person, one genuine sanyasi, and I'll concede that I was wrong and you were right! Take a month. Search hard. But you won't find a genuine man of God in this godforsaken city!'

Birbal began his search for a genuine sanyasi in a light-hearted frame of mind. The task seemed far easier than so many others the Emperor had given him. If he could sell a worthless piece of rope for three hundred gold *mohurs,* what was so difficult about locating one genuine man of God?

The days passed and Birbal met innumerable fakirs and sadhus. But when he honestly asked himself if they were genuine sanyasis, the answer was always 'No'. Some trace of greed, or arrogance, or dishonesty was always present in the so-called men of God that he encountered.

The last day of the month arrived. There was just one more ashram he had to visit on the outskirts of the city. Birbal went there without much hope. And sure enough, the holy men he met there turned out to be no more holy than him. 'What do I do now?' Birbal asked himself in exasperation, 'short of dressing myself in ochre robes and posing as a genuine sanyasi for the benefit of the Emperor?'

As he walked away from the ashram, he heard someone singing softly. It was a young lad scrubbing dirty utensils in a corner of the courtyard, totally absorbed in his task. Birbal stopped for a moment to watch him.

The boy looked up. His face was as fresh, as pure, and as innocent as the dawn of a new day. Something clicked in Birbal's brain ...

He presented himself in the *diwan-i-khas* the following evening.

'Well, Birbal,' said the Emperor, 'how many genuine sanyasis have you found for me?'

'Your Majesty was right,' said Birbal. 'There were hardly any. But I did find one! Perhaps Your Majesty would like to visit his humble abode?'

'Most certainly,' said the Emperor.

Early the following morning, Birbal led Akbar to a lonely stretch of ground beside the river Yamuna.

There, beneath a tree, sat the young servant from the ashram, wearing the ochre garments of a sadhu that Birbal had got for him.

'Sit as if you are meditating,' Birbal had coached the boy carefully the previous afternoon. 'You have seen the sadhus in the ashram meditating, or pretending to meditate. Sit like them with your eyes closed. Open your eyes if someone addresses you, but don't say anything or you will give the game away! If anyone offers you anything, don't take it —don't even look at it! Just pretend to be a sanyasi who is not interested in anything that the world can offer. If you do a good job of pretending, I'll reward you so well you won't need to scrub utensils ever again!'

Birbal's heart was beating fast as he and the Emperor approached the fake sanyasi.

'He is very young,' the Emperor said softly. 'But look at the glow on his face!'

It was true. The boy was acting perfectly. He looked every inch a true saint, utterly absorbed in thoughts of God, and God alone.

Akbar and Birbal stood before him with folded hands for a long time. Then Akbar gently placed a bag full of gold *mohurs* at his feet. The boy opened his eyes and looked calmly at the Emperor. Not once did he glance at the bag of gold *mohurs*. Or at the priceless necklace of diamonds and rubies the Emperor removed from his own neck and placed in the dust beside the bag of gold *mohurs*. A fortune lay at his feet, but the young boy ignored it and continued to sit peacefully in meditation.

Many more minutes passed before the Emperor stirred. 'Our gifts are worthless before the inner riches this young saint has found,' he said. 'My kingdom is blessed by his presence. The peace he radiates has cleansed and calmed my troubled mind. Let us not disturb his meditation any longer. Birbal, I am happy I was wrong and you were right. There is at least one genuinely holy man in the city of Agra!'

Picking up the bag of gold *mohurs* and the diamond and ruby necklace, Birbal followed the Emperor back to the palace.

He returned as soon as he could, exulting inwardly. The young servant had done a wonderful job of convincing the Emperor!

'Enough!' he said to the boy, who was still sitting with his eyes closed. 'There is no more need to pretend. You did a fine job, and here are the fifty *mohurs* I promised you.'

The boy looked at the bag of mohurs but made no move to take it from Birbal.

'Isn't it enough?' asked Birbal, a little annoyed. 'Don't be greedy now. I am not the Emperor.'

The boy was lost in his own thoughts. There was a strange look on his face as if he had made a great discovery.

'I don't want the money,' he said. 'Thanks to your great kindness, I became a sanyasi in the eyes of the Emperor. He laid a fortune at my feet even though I was only a fake sanyasi!'

The boy looked at Birbal earnestly—his eyes were shining. 'Imagine the riches that could be mine if I became a real sanyasi! Not the riches of this world, but the inner riches the Emperor spoke about—the inner riches God showers on those who seek Him, and Him alone.'

He bent to touch Birbal's feet in gratitude and farewell. 'Pray for me,' he said. 'Pray that I may find a guru to guide me in my search for God.'

Gently, Birbal raised him up. 'I will pray for you, my son,' he said. 'And I know my prayer will be answered.'

There was a smile on Birbal's lips as he set off homeward. He'd thought he had fooled the Emperor, but he had not. God be praised, there was indeed at least one genuine sanyasi in the kingdom, even if he was just beginning his spiritual journey!

The Man Who Never Belched

The Emperor had just partaken of a very satisfying meal at Birbal's house. 'That was an excellent meal, Birbal!' he said. 'I have seldom tasted such delicious *saag*. I should tell my *mir bahawal* to borrow your cook for a few weeks.'

The Emperor and his retinue stepped out of Birbal's house into the clear, cool November night. 'Birbal, let us take a walk, to remove the ill effects of a heavy meal,' Akbar said.

Birbal nodded. 'It is a beautiful night, Your

Majesty,' he said trying unsuccessfully to suppress a belch.

'Polluted by your bad manners,' hissed Mulla do Piaza to Birbal.

Akbar heard the whisper. 'Come, my good Mulla,' he said. 'You are unduly harsh on your host. What you just called bad manners is something natural to every man!'

'I beg to disagree, Alampanah,' said Mulla do Piaza coldly. 'I, for one, never made such a rude noise in all my life!'

Birbal inclined his head in mock politeness and said, 'My friend, you are a better person than I am.' His sarcasm escaped Mulla do Piaza completely.

A few days passed by. Then one day Akbar was up all night discussing and planning a new campaign. By dawn, he was weary and cramped after sitting for so long.

'I shall take a short walk to stretch my legs, and then I must retire for my prayers,' he said to Birbal, laying his hand on Birbal's shoulder.

'Follow me, My Lord,' said Birbal, 'and I shall show you a sight to gladden your heart.'

'Lead the way, Birbal,' said Akbar.

Birbal led the king towards the Buland Darwaza of Fatehpur Sikri. Up ahead, streams of water rose upward from a beautiful fountain, pink and orange roses lined the dusty path. The roses swayed gently with the wind, presenting a lovely sight. On almost every upturned petal, a dewdrop glistened like a brilliant pearl.

'Allah be praised!' said the Emperor devoutly. 'How beautiful are his creations! Look, Birbal, don't these dewdrops look like pearls?'

Akbar was just about to touch one of the petals, when Birbal said, 'They are pearls, My Lord, but—I humbly beg your pardon—not for you and me. If we touch them, they are mere dewdrops. But for someone pure, someone unblemished, someone who has never made a rude noise in all his life—for such a rare person, My Lord, these pearls remain pearls!'

Akbar was astonished at first but he soon got Birbal's point. Trying to keep as straight a face as possible, he said, 'A person such as you describe is hard to find... But wait—' Then turning to Mulla do Piaza he said, 'My dear fellow, the night we dined at Birbal's house, did you not say that you had never belched in your life? You are the rare and unblemished man that Birbal is talking about! For you these are pearls, not dewdrops. Stretch out your hand and gather them!'

Mulla do Piaza stood transfixed to the ground.

'There are enough pearls here to string a thousand necklaces!' Birbal smirked. 'Why do you hesitate?'

Mulla do Piaza remained silent. But if looks could kill, Birbal would have been dead that very instant. Once again, he had outwitted the angry Mulla.

The Test

One morning a tall, slim youth with a confident bearing bowed low before Emperor Akbar in the *diwan-e-aam*.

'Jahanpanah,' he said, 'I have studied Persian and Turki, as well as Sanskrit. I also have some knowledge of statecraft and philosophy.'

'You seem to be a very talented young man,' remarked the Emperor, looking at him keenly. Akbar wondered why the youth looked familiar. He went on, 'We are always in need of able men. The royal hen house needs a good worker. It has been badly neglected. The job is yours if you want it.'

The young man was shocked! He had hoped for a position among the Emperor's courtiers, not among his hens and chickens! Hiding his disappointment, he bowed again and said, 'Your Majesty, I will take up my duties from tomorrow.'

Two months went by. One afternoon, the Emperor decided to inspect the royal hen house. He found it clean and tidy. The hens looked healthy and well-fed.

'These hens look very prosperous,' Akbar observed to the recently-employed youth. 'You must be spending a great deal of money on their food.'

'Not at all, Your Majesty,' said the young man quickly. 'There is enough left over everyday from the royal kitchen to feed them well.'

'Is that so?' said Akbar. 'You have done a good job. My library is as neglected as this hen house was until you put it right. Look after the library from tomorrow.'

If the young man was disappointed once again, he did not show it. The following day he started his new assignment. Emperor Akbar's library contained thousands of manuscripts that lay in dusty heaps. The young man set to work ...

Two months passed before the Emperor found

time to visit the royal library. It had been transformed into a clean and airy room! Each manuscript lay enclosed in a handsome cover of velvet.

Akbar gasped! 'Amazing!' he said. 'But how much did you spend from the royal treasury on all this velvet?'

'Nothing at all, Your Majesty,' said the young man eagerly. 'Hundreds of petitions reach your court every day. They are enclosed in velvet covers, which are then discarded. I have merely been collecting these discarded covers to cover these manuscripts, with a little help from the royal tailor.'

'You have done very well! Very well indeed! You have proved your worth. Come to the court tomorrow. Let us see if your knowledge of languages, statecraft, and philosophy—I remember all your accomplishments—equals your knowledge of kitchen leftovers and dusty manuscripts!'

Smiling broadly, Akbar left the library, satisfied that his court had gained a deserving new courtier.

'But why does the boy's face look familiar? I cannot understand it, Birbal,' said Akbar, after relating the entire story of the young man to him later that night. Birbal had been away from Agra for many months, on an assignment for the Emperor.

'Your Majesty,' said Birbal, 'perhaps the boy's face looks familiar because he looks like me. He is my younger brother.'

'Your brother, Birbal? But why didn't you tell me this before? I may not then have tested him the way I did!'

'That is why I stayed silent, Your Majesty,' said Birbal. 'Although I was away much of the time, I kept track of what was happening. My brother has many talents …'

'Like you, Birbal,' murmured the Emperor.

'Your Majesty, you flatter your humble servant. My brother is talented, but he was becoming a little overconfident, a little arrogant. Your Majesty has knocked that out of him, and he will be the better for having had to prove his worth.'

'Two Birbals to contend with!' The Emperor raised his eyebrows in mock alarm. 'Handling a charging elephant or an angry tigress may be easier!'

Birbal hid a smile as the Emperor's laughter rang through the silent night.

Journey to Heaven

One morning Akbar was being attended to as usual by the royal barber. As the barber's fingers moved skillfully over Akbar's face he asked, 'Jahanpanah, if I may be bold enough to enquire, do you not sometimes miss your late father, our glorious Emperor?'

'I miss him often,' said Akbar pensively. 'Death robbed me early of his guidance.'

'Would Your Majesty not like to know how your great father is faring in heaven?' continued the barber.

'If only that were possible,' murmured Akbar with a smile.

A few days later, when some courtiers were also present, the barber brought up the subject again. 'Shah Alam, last night I was greatly blessed. I saw His Royal Highness, your late father in my dream,' he lied.

'Is that so?' said Akbar. 'I hope His Majesty was in good health.'

'He was, Jahanpanah,' said the barber. 'But he was alone and seemed to be in need of company. That perturbed me.'

A frown creased Akbar's brow.

'Jahanpanah, may I make a suggestion?' said Shahbaz Khan. 'Perhaps there is a way to lighten His Majesty's solitude. Someone who is both wise and witty could be sent to paradise to keep his Royal Highness company.'

'Hmmm! And who do you think would be most suitable for such an honour?' Akbar wondered if another plot was being hatched against his favourite courtier. His suspicion was confirmed when the barber said eagerly, 'Raja Birbal, above all others, in my humble opinion.'

Shahbaz Khan and Mulla do Piaza nodded their heads in agreement.

'And no harm would come to him, Your Majesty,'

continued the barber. 'There is a magician in Agra who regularly sends people to heaven and gets them back alive!'

'Do you think your Emperor is foolish enough to believe such a story?' thought Akbar. 'Old man, it seems there is as much greed in your heart as there is skill in your fingers. How much were you paid for trying to trap Birbal?'

But Akbar's face did not betray his thoughts. 'Send for Birbal,' was all he said.

Later that day Birbal heard the proposal to dispatch him to paradise.

'Well! What have you to say?' asked Akbar. Silently he added, 'Find a way to save yourself, my friend.'

Birbal bowed. His face was expressionless. 'Jahanpanah, what could be a greater honour for me than to serve His Royal Highness in heaven? But I beg leave for a month to prepare for my journey.'

'Granted,' said the Emperor. Mulla do Piaza and Shahbaz Khan glanced at each other in delight.

Birbal's departure for heaven was to take place in a large field not far from his home. A huge pyre of straw and wood was to be set alight and Birbal was to rise to heaven with the smoke from the fire. He himself selected the exact spot and supervised all the arrangements.

A month passed. On the appointed day, Emperor Akbar and his courtiers watched as Birbal mounted the pyre. He asked for extra straw to be piled all over him so as to make the fire even bigger and brighter. The magician brought by the barber began to recite spells that would ensure Birbal's safe journey to heaven. The pyre was lit. Sick at heart, Akbar wondered why Birbal had not saved himself. The Emperor despaired of ever seeing his friend again …

But Birbal had not gone up to heaven with the smoke from the raging fire. Instead, as soon as the pyre was lit, he had gone down into a tunnel that he had had dug secretly all the way to his home nearby!

Exactly three months later Birbal reappeared in court. His hair had grown long and there was a beard on his face.

'Birbal!' exclaimed Akbar joyfully. 'Is it really you? When did you return from heaven?'

'I have just returned, Your Majesty,' said Birbal, bowing deeply. 'And I am happy to report that His Royal Highness, your esteemed father, is in good health and spirits.'

'We are delighted to hear that,' said Akbar.

'His Royal Highness enjoys every comfort in paradise,' Birbal went on. 'Just one thing is lacking. And that is the reason for my return and my appearance. Your Majesty, there are no barbers in heaven. Your father requests you to send him a skilled barber as soon as possible.'

Akbar concealed a smile. How cleverly had Birbal turned the tables on those who sought to kill him!

'We will send His Highness the best barber in the land this very day!' declared Akbar. 'Let the royal barber prepare for his journey to heaven!'

The Questions

Late one evening, when Birbal entered the *diwan-i-khas*, an odd silence greeted him. Something else was odd too. Those courtiers, who normally met him with a scornful look or a snide remark, were looking at him hopefully. Then Birbal saw a stranger seated by himself, with a covered copper pot in front of him. Perhaps he was the reason for their strange behaviour …

Akbar's voice broke into Birbal's thoughts. 'An envoy from His Majesty, the ruler of Kabul, has graced our court,' said the Emperor. 'He has heard glowing reports of the knowledge and the talent of our courtiers and he wishes to ask them a few simple questions.'

'We are deeply honoured,' murmured Birbal, bowing to the stranger.

'I repeat my question,' said the stranger, looking arrogantly at the assembled courtiers. 'Who can tell me what is in this pot?'

None of the courtiers were willing to meet his gaze.

'What could it be?' whispered Raja Todar Mal to Mulla do Piaza.

'Dry fruit perhaps,' muttered the Mulla. 'He comes from Kabul.'

'That would be too easy an answer,' hissed Shahbaz Khan.

'Precious stones, a length of fine silk, gold mohurs … The pot could be full of anything!' whispered Shadi Shah. 'How are we to know?'

'Now that he has come, let Birbal put his head in the noose,' said Mulla do Piaza softly. 'Let him answer this impossible question. Who knows, by some fluke, he may guess the right answer!'

'*Huzoor*, if you have no objection, may I examine the pot a little closely?' Birbal addressed the stranger.

'By all means,' said the envoy coolly. He shrugged

his shoulders. 'The task we have set is not difficult.'

The courtiers looked uneasily at one another while Birbal walked over to the pot and bent down to examine it. Then with a sudden movement, he whipped off the cloth loosely covering the mouth of the pot, and peered inside.

'The pot is full of—emptiness, Your Honour!' declared Birbal. 'It contains nothing!'

'But … but,' the envoy was spluttering with anger, 'you were not supposed to uncover the pot and look inside!'

'*Huzoor*, you said nothing about not uncovering the pot,' Birbal said innocently. 'In fact you gave me permission to examine it more closely!'

Akbar hid a smile. Birbal had proved his ingenuity once again.

'Your Majesty, I have more questions,' said the envoy, still glowering at Birbal. 'One–where is the centre of the earth? Two–how many stars are there in the sky?'

For a moment the entire court gaped at the envoy. Birbal was the first to recover his composure.

'These are profound questions, Your Honour,' he said. The envoy looked complacent. 'And we would need some time to answer them.'

'I am in your country for another ten days,' said the envoy grandly.

'We will have the answers ready before your departure,' said Birbal with a respectful bow.

'And till then you are our honoured guest,' Akbar said to the envoy. 'Enjoy the beauties and the wonders of our kingdom!'

For the next nine days Birbal absented himself from court. No one knew how he was preparing to answer the envoy's questions.

On the tenth and last evening of the envoy's visit, at Birbal's request, the Emperor and the courtiers gathered outside the *diwan-i-khas*. Birbal bowed to the envoy.

'Thanks to your first question,' he said, 'we have made a stupendous discovery!' He pointed to a mark he had made on the ground. 'Here! Right here is the centre of the earth! And we are fortunate enough to be standing on it!'

He turned to the dumbfounded envoy. 'All our research and consultations with experts have revealed this truth. You are of course, welcome to verify it.'

'Of course,' echoed the envoy in a faint voice. Behind him both Birbal's friends and foes grinned at one another. 'And the answer to my second question?'

Birbal signalled to one of the guards, and in a minute six sheep were brought before the assembly.

'*Huzoor*,' said Birbal to the envoy, 'your second question was—how many stars are there in the sky?

Again a very difficult question, *huzoor*, but here is the answer. There are exactly as many stars in the sky as there are hairs on these six sheep! It was not easy to locate sheep with the exact number of hairs, and that too in ten days, but by God's grace we were able to do it!'

Once again the envoy was at a loss for words. 'But wh-what is the actual number of stars in the sky?' he stammered.

'You did not explicitly ask for a number, *huzoor*,' Birbal said patiently. 'You merely expressed a desire to know how many stars there are in the sky and we have answered your question. However, if you also wish to know the exact number, I am sure a verification of our claim would provide it.'

The envoy knew he had been defeated. Over his sullen head, the Emperor's eyes met Birbal's, full of laughter and admiration.

Once again Birbal had proved that he was truly inimitable!

The Two Merchants

Birbal was known for his keen intelligence, his fair-mindedness and his proximity to the Emperor. Citizens seeking justice often came to Birbal, particularly when Akbar was away from the city.

In one particular instance, Birbal was trying to resolve a dispute between two merchants. 'So you have no proof of what you are saying?' Birbal asked the first merchant.

'No *huzoor*,' said the merchant. His name was Ram Chand.

'No written receipt for the fifteen hundred rupees that you say you lent your friend Jwala Prasad? And no witness to the transaction?'

'No *huzoor*,' said Ram Chand again. 'Jwala Prasad is a fellow merchant as well as a friend. He needed the money and promised to return it within six months. So I lent it to him. I thought he would honour his word. But he refuses even to remember what happened.'

'Write down all that you have told me and sign it,' said Birbal. 'I will see what I can do.'

Birbal then sent for Jwala Prasad, the second merchant. Jwala Prasad bustled into Birbal's presence looking very pleased, bowed low and said, 'Raja Sahib, I am deeply honoured and grateful for this summons. How may I be of service to Your Lordship?'

'Read this,' said Birbal and handed him Ram Chand's written statement. The merchant paled a little as he read it. But he said with great assurance, 'All lies! Your Lordship, all lies! I thought Ram Chand was my friend. I have helped him so many times. And this is how he repays me!' He shook his head sadly. 'I know his shop is not doing well, but this is not the way …'

'So you deny that Ram Chand lent you fifteen hundred rupees which you promised to return within six months?' said Birbal.

'I absolutely deny it, Your Honour,' said Jwala Prasad solemnly. 'And surely he would have taken a receipt from me if he had lent me such a large sum. Why does he not produce that receipt?'

'He says he did not take a receipt,' said Birbal. 'That is the problem. Thank you for coming. I am sorry for wasting your time.'

'Raja Sahib, I am your humble servant.' Jwala Prasad folded his hands, bowed and took his leave.

A few days later Birbal sent both the merchants a large tin of ghee each with a request that they sell the ghee for him after checking its purity. On heating the ghee both Ram Chand and Jwala Prasad discovered a gold *mohur* at the bottom of the tin.

Ram Chand promptly returned the *mohur* to Birbal, saying it must have fallen into the ghee by mistake. Jwala Prasad handed the *mohur* that he had found to his son who helped him in their shop.

'Keep this safely,' he said, 'till I ask for it.'

When the two merchants had sold the ghee that Birbal had sent them, they went back to give him the money from the sale. Birbal took the money from Ram Chand, thanked him and sent him away. Jwala Prasad appeared later with a smaller amount of money.

'Is that the best price you could get for one and a

half *maunds* of ghee?' asked Birbal.

'Your Lordship, the tin only contained one *maund*,' protested Jwala Prasad. 'I weighed it before I heated the ghee. My son was with me.'

'Then my men may have made a mistake,' said Birbal. 'Please wait while I find out.'

He went inside and told one of his servants to go to Jwala Prasad's house and fetch his son. 'Tell him that his father wants him to bring the gold *mohur* that he found at the bottom of the tin of ghee,' said Birbal.

In a short while the servant returned with the boy. Jwala Prasad was taken aback to see his son.

'Have you brought the gold *mohur*?' Birbal asked.

'Yes,' said the boy and pulled it out of his pocket.

'Weren't there two *mohurs* in the tin of ghee?' Birbal enquired with an air of innocence.

'No, Your Honour,' replied the boy. 'We found just one.'

Jwala Prasad looked most uncomfortable. 'What nonsense are you talking?' he snapped at his son. 'What would a gold *mohur* be doing in a tin of ghee?'

'But don't you remember?' The boy asked his father in surprise. 'We found the *mohur* in the tin when we heated the ghee. You took the *mohur* out and gave it to me for safekeeping.'

'Yes, yes! I remember I gave you a *mohur*,' said

Jwala Prasad hurriedly. 'But it didn't come out of any tin. One of my customers gave it to me.'

'Your son is telling the truth, Jwala Prasad,' said Birbal. 'I put the gold *mohur* in the tin myself to see what you would do with it.'

Jwala Prasad was sweating with fear but he still tried to bluff his way out.

'My memory must be playing tricks on me, Your Honour,' he said. 'Please forgive me.' He turned to his son. 'Give the gold *mohur* to his lordship at once! How can we keep what doesn't belong to us?'

'And when do you propose to return the fifteen hundred rupees you borrowed from your friend Ram Chand?' enquired Birbal, taking the *mohur*.

'Haven't you returned that money yet?' the merchant's son asked his father anxiously.

'Be quiet!' Jwala Prasad hissed at the boy. But he knew the game was up!

'Don't rebuke your son,' said Birbal sternly. 'He is an honest lad and he will make a better merchant than you. Now follow his example and tell me the truth.'

Seeing there was no way out, Jwala Prasad confessed. As a penalty, Birbal made him give Ram Chand double the amount that he had borrowed from him. Jwala Prasad also returned the money he owed Birbal for half a *maund* of ghee.

'If such a dishonest man can still have an honest son,' thought Birbal as father and son departed, 'then God be praised, there is still hope for humanity!'

The Green Horse

Emperor Akbar had been on a long and successful hunting trip. The trained cheetahs who accompanied him pursued and brought down some of the fastest deer in the forest. The Emperor himself, who was a fine shot, had bagged a wily stag that had long eluded him.

Now he was relaxing with a few courtiers in the palace gardens. Green leafy trees and lush green grass soothed both his mind and body.

'Green is the most beautiful and restful of all

colours,' declared the Emperor.

'It is, Your Majesty,' echoed the courtiers.

'If only Allah had created a green horse!' mused Akbar aloud. 'One would ride him for hours and not get fatigued!'

Mulla do Piaza and Shahbaz Khan looked at each other. Here was another chance perhaps to get the better of Birbal.

'Alampanah,' said Mullah do Piaza with an air of innocence, 'the world is full of wonders. A green horse may well exist! And who but our infinitely resourceful friend Birbal to seek him out?'

The Emperor knew, as did everyone present, that there was no such animal as a green horse. But Birbal had been challenged once again by those who envied and resented him. And Akbar was curious to see how Birbal would meet this challenge.

'Well, Birbal?' he said. 'Do you think you can find a green horse for your Emperor?'

'Jahanpanah, if such a unique and fortunate beast exists, rest assured that I will find him,' replied Birbal. 'Grant me two weeks to fulfil my task.'

'I thought the Emperor was an intelligent man!' said Birbal's wife when she heard what had happened.

'He is!' said Birbal. 'He is waiting to see how I am going to use *my* intelligence!'

'Why don't you just colour a white horse green

and take it to him?' she suggested.

'Now you are insulting both the Emperor's intelligence as well as mine,' said Birbal, smiling. 'Do you think he would not see through such a trick? And in any case I don't believe in cruelty to animals. Don't worry, this problem, like all other problems, will have a solution.'

Two weeks later a bright and cheerful Birbal presented himself in court.

'Your Majesty,' he said, bowing deeply, 'I have found the only green horse in the world and its owner is ready to sell the horse to you on two conditions.'

'That is wonderful news!' said the Emperor. 'What are the conditions? Let him demand the highest price for his precious horse and we will pay it.'

'Your Majesty, his first condition is that you should go to him yourself to buy the horse.'

'That condition is easily fulfilled,' said Akbar. 'What is the second condition?'

'Jahanpanah, he says the horse he is willing to sell you is no ordinary animal. So, no ordinary day will do for the sale of such an animal. If Your Majesty approaches him on any other day besides the seven days of the week, he will be more than happy to oblige you!'

For a few moments, there was pin-drop silence as the entire assembly absorbed the meaning of

Birbal's words. Then the Emperor burst out laughing. Once again, Birbal had outwitted his rivals.

'You are priceless!' Akbar said affectionately. 'No green horse could be as priceless!'

Read more in the **Wise Men of the East** series from Scholastic:

The Wisdom of Mulla Nasruddin
Shahrukh Husain

In a small town somewhere in the Middle East lived Mulla Nasruddin. Mulla Nasruddin was famous for being a bit odd. He reacted to the follies of his fellow men and to the challenges of daily life—be it catching a runaway basket or celebrating the birth of a pot— in a manner that people found strange. But most wise men agreed that beneath the apparent foolishness of Mulla Nasruddin was a keen perception that cut straight to the truth.

This collection of twenty-five tales contains all the fun and wisdom that make the stories of Mulla Nasruddin so widely read and well loved.

Read more in the **Wise Men of the East** series from Scholastic:

The Wit of Tenali Raman
Devika Rangachari

Everyone agreed that Raman of Tenali was very clever. As a boy, he exasperated people with his mischief just as much as he impressed them with his intelligence. As jester in the court of King Krishna Devaraya, Tenali continued to entertain and annoy the king and courtiers in equal measure. But underlying the buffoonery and audacious exploits was a keen concern for truth and a desire to bring to light the follies of men and society.

This collection of eighteen stories contains all the wit and wisdom that make the stories of Tenali Raman so widely read and well loved.